I0519721

Fear Naught
The Junk Drawer of Poetry

Owen Patterson

BREVIS Publishing ■ Chicago

Sky co-opted
Earth compromised
Brick and mortar
The co-operative order
Timberland kindled, blazed, and flash
Reduce to cinders... haze, and ash
The Greek Wanderer, aflame
As heavens pass by
Icarus wanes... and does not fly

He need not reach for the sun

Planētēs Naught
(πλανήτης Ø)

Titles by Owen Patterson

The Dis-condition of Ease (prose fiction, 2015)

Lovely Faze (poetry, 2017)

Stars at Naught (poetry, 2018)

Jaded (poetry, 2018)

Fear Naught
The Junk Drawer of Poetry (poetry/prose, 2019)

See online book reviews at *Windy City Reviews*

BREVIS Publishing, Chicago, IL USA 2019
ISBN: 978-0-9964834-6-9 (BREVIS); **EDIT x8.92**

Formatting by Owen Patterson
Cover design by "Pica"; Edmund Barca
Cover photos by Owen Patterson
Editing by Gallus "Giblet" Morsél

Special Thanks:
Yasmeen Patterson Ahmad, Edmund Barca Gaylord, Florentina Lona, Gallus Morsél, Sorina Simona Savin

Thanks for your advice and help.

For Karin Janine

CONTENTS

Creation
and creativity
and nature
and love
and straight lines
and circle backs
missings and misgivings
and longings
and love agains
and purposes
and...
Creation

Circle Backs

Flow

Purely... Voice

The sun rises... somewhere,
over gentle hillsides, arrayed
with wildflowers, lavender,
and warm thoughts.

Happy 14th

we precipitate

flow and create
seasons change crystal lattice, to rain
sweat beads upon bodies, that heat
mist and steam raise
clouded dreams

engorged... 'till deluge

we precipitate
we create

flow and create

You are fluid
I am a rock
If I fall into your stream
you will go around me
I imagine that, over time
you will wear down my rough edges
I will become, smooth
but you will still
just go around

pebbles and flow

Wrong turn
Lost in curves
Winding roads
Swing to and fro
Back and forth
Back and forth
To your door
Knocked and knocked
And knocked some more
Upon hardwood rapped
Less subtle than tapped
More trouble than that
Abode entrance granting
Senses spent
And I left panting

Spent and Panting

Lips, that kiss the universe
Eyes, that pierce darkness
Mind, that perceives beyond

Love The

No se preocupe tanto, bella dama
Si olvido su cabello
Recodaré sus ojos
Y si también los olvido
Recodaré sus labios
Y si olvido los todos esos
Soñaré con las cosas desconocidas
Que todavía no he visto

Soñar Con La Bella Dama

Don't worry so much, beautiful lady
If I forget your hair
I will remember your eyes
And if also I forget those
I will remember your lips
And if I forget *all* of those
I will dream of the unknown things
That I have not yet seen

Soñar Con La Bella Dama
To Dream of the Beautiful Lady

My Love, never I possesses
Neither sold nor bartered for
My Love, gives I of self
Without condition conscripted

Poetry I, My Love

Silence Tucked Into Clamor

So many moths
Such a beautiful flame
So much ash

Fall to Ash

Abandoned homes and buildings...
Look beyond...
See the abandoned people...

Abandoned

Barrage of
Ones in a million
Is ones in a billion
Faces, lost in montage

Shards cut
To fit, collage

One
Lost in twenty
Painful
Awkward
Silence tucked into clamor

Shards and edges
That no longer touch

Windy chimes
That no longer sound

Windy Chimes

To say, "this is real; as real as anything."
This, is an odd statement
for one that routinely questions reality

To go from ropes in trees
to bullets in streets...

To go from children's books and colored pages...
to sad looks in child sized cages...

To shuffle babies into strangers' homes...
The Shady Maybes...
to mothers' tears shown...

When indifference is reality
no wonder...
the one that questions...
The Shady Maybes

Shady Maybes

sinuous chatter
words meander past
right angles
scarcely balanced between
obtuse and acute

the sinuous chatter
of serpentine matters
as riverbed snakes
erode resettle replace

shifting contexts
bear witness to falsehoods

shifting contexts

Monster among angels
Cherubs take flight
Dodge raging fire spit

And fire spit falls and fails

Monster among monsters
Demons turn mocking

Fire spit blossom
Red of rose falls, and fails

Faux monster, displaced
Lost between
Cherubs and demons

Faux Monster Limbo

Fisheye bowl
As I rise
Blood boils, bends partly
This party never ends
Never dies
Fisheye bowl
And as I smile
Blood boils my soul, partly
This party ever flows
Never dies
And I smile

Fisheye Bowl

Crash

Metal hot
Glass shatter
Blood splatter

Thought
When woke
Body whole?

Yes, body whole
'Twas jade
That broke

Good Luck

Why morn?
The Unarmed Urban Unicorn
Not even a hint
Non-existent
Not to solve them
Not a problem
Why morn?
Why the scorn?
Why do you speak?
Why block the street?
Too many shots hit

"Tonto quick
Pass another clip"

"Kemosabe! Shit!
Unarmed Urban Unicorn!"

U.U.U.

Art in Life

Yes, truth matters.
Writing can be fiction...
yet, remain genuine.

Sparks and light
Spots, hottest white
And coolest black

Essence between...
Of contrast photography
Where mysteries, arise
And life is found, in art

Essence of Image

senses gave birth to image
that gave birth to shared concept
that gave birth to word
and full circle...
word offers purple tree
that liberates concept
that inspires image
that stirs senses

...and full circle

It was the best of times.

Jerry laughed the night away. The alternative was death.

"Will there be cookies?"

"Cookies?"

"You know… comfort food."

"Did you actually like the cookies?"

"I liked the cookie maker… cups of warm milk and honey… the strong hand holding at my back… the softest lips pressed my forehead… a smile so intense that I would swear it was a laugh…"

Karin and Jerry shared the full range of life. She assured him, "Yes, I suppose… we all need cookies."

Jerry relaxed. He was prepared for whatever fate might bring.

The Cookie Maker

Memoir, Word To The Younger Self

Transplanted young man... lands, with a thud. '80s Fort Wayne, far more segregated than expected; even more so than, his beloved Chicago... Fort Wayne, a town so sad... so many, go about their days, not smiling in public...

Young Chicago transplant... don't smile... don't smile... You may want to smile, as now I smile, but don't smile... You'll stand out. The others, they don't like that. Don't smile...

Late night study sessions at the 24 hour Arby's, turn to early morning playings of the dozens... Brains fatigued by numbers, equations, and charts. You all roll, far away from the serious, all the way to the silly.

Transplanted young man... you're not an engineer. Hear me! You are a poet! Hear me! You're not listening, are you? You are forgetting the sad little town. You all, are smiling. Don't smile... don't smile... You'll stand out.

Transplanted young man... you may hear my, "don't smile" and think me a coward, but truth... I worry for you. See the troopers file in... jovial comrades, smile and joke... fill the Arby's, for their late night, shift break... See their smiles cease... and become well-practiced scowls, as their attention turns toward you. Hands on firearm grips, with intent, to intimidate... Long barrels and large calibers, combat rural backroad traffickers... Of which, you are none.

The silly, rolls all the way back, to the serious, as you all stand, and exit. Young Chicago transplant... don't smile... don't smile... You may want to smile, as now I smile, but don't smile... You'll stand out. And the others, they don't like that. Don't smile...

Pennies and Faith

When I was in school, we discussed free will vs predetermination. An omniscient god would know our future actions. In such a case, we would not have free will. Our paths would be predetermined. We would be unable to change what God has already seen to be true. For humans to have free will, God would have to choose to not see our paths. We would then be free to make true choices. I only mention this to express that God can also make choices.

An omnipotent god *could* create a rock heavier than She could lift. Perhaps the rock would be designed to infinitely increase in weight just ahead of Her own strength. But to what end? To prove that it could be done; to satisfy human curiosity? It seems to me, that to do such a thing would be the act of a very insecure god. I don't believe that She would choose to do this. To be honest, I don't really know. I am finite… mostly.

Faith is belief in that which cannot be proven. Some things are factual and don't require faith. One penny plus one penny equals two pennies; that's a fact. I love my children and I believe that you love your children. I would have a difficult time proving my love or your love, but I have faith.

Paradox

by definition... absurd

Emily…

Dead poet
Great poet

Dead before her time
Great before ever…

"Discovered"

Emily…

Lo…
Behold
Rise the sun

Light rays slice chilled air
Through kitchen windows
Moments of… blinded eyes
And radiated faces
Warmth bestowed
Upon touch

Cold rooms
Before stoves' early fires
Goosed flesh accounts
Reminders of… spectacle
Of… wonders
And morning miracles

Warmth bestowed
Upon touch
I am blessed

Warmth Bestowed

So courageous!
So brave!

Yeah
I wouldn't say that to you

Start the day
Open your eyes
Brush your hair
Wash the skin
That you're in
Greet the world
Just the same
As the day you were born

Walk out
Into your soul
Into your spirit
Into your person

So courageous!
So brave!

How silly would I be?
How silly a thing *should* it be?
To say...
Congratulations!
For just being yourself

Yeah
I won't say it

But I really really want to

Congratulations!

The smile is fallacious
Gracious the demeanor
The limp belies corporal breaks

Confident stride
Determined
Ready to fight
Always ready to give
As well as one gets

Empathy germinates
In soils of
Contrary circumstance

Contrary Circumstance

She thinks people are ridiculous
in their simplicity. Yet, she longs
for simplicity of quiet, beautiful
compositions, of old masters.
Oh, the irony of paradox...

Absurd Truth

Atoms...
Facts of matter
Mostly empty

Lattice patterns
Crystal platters
Through ladder thistles
Thimbles like forests
Porous timbers
More us trees
Winds whistle
'Round colander cymbals

Atoms...
Facts of matter
Mostly empty

Facts of Matter

Posts

Uh... OK.

At times,
I do engage in
a wee bit of smartass-ery.

665.99…

The Almost Beastie

So... wtf is *not*
"Where's the food?"
I have to go back
and edit a few comments.

WTF

"Is that kale?"

"No, I think it's grass."

"No! It's kale!"

"Le' me see! Le' me see!"

"You guys are idiots. I'm outta here."

Lógos, The Black Sheep
(λόγος το μαύρο πρόβατο)

I am... a cause without any rebels.

As Gran'pa used to say…
"Crazy's like cinnamon; too much
ruins the pie."

"The Muppets... they love me."

"Make Sesame Street Great Again!"

"I'm going to build a wall, and Plaza Sésamo is going to pay for it!"

Fondald the Grump

You sir... are a donkey's anus!

"Hey Kermit... stop complaining about being Green. I'm the one that's driving, and I'm Brown!"

-Fozzie Bear

If one does not treat others as human,
it does not call into question the others' humanity.
It questions that of the one.

Inhuman

A hammer…
Everything looks like a nail

A handgun…
Everything looks like…

Looks Like…

Even when there were those
who did not believe Earth was round...
it was still round.

Whether one believes or not...
change ever approaches.

Deniers

It's hard for me to imagine art without nature.

"The heart of gold shall never tarnish."

– Florentina Lona - *Heart*

Love can't buy you money,
but there are always
good times to be had.

Can't Buy It

[She comments]
A writer's imaginative reality must be a fun place. Is it not, Owen? 😆
[I react: Haha 😄]

[I comment]
Yes... fun, but also weird. Any possible thing that we image, has happened somewhere, is happening, or will happen. When I was young, I was always skeptical of my writing. I thought that I was plagiarizing things that I had read, but had forgotten. Or that someone was projecting stories into my mind. It was a long time before I trusted my creativity. Even now, I don't completely consider my writing my own. It's part of a collective creative continuum.
[She reacts: Love 🖤]

[I comment/I paraphrase]
Leviticus 25:23...
[Creation] shall not be sold. Ever [Creation] belongs to [The Infinite]. You are [in need of shelter] and you are [an impermanent visitor in Creation] with [The Infinite].
[She reacts: Haha 😄]

Posting Prose Poetic

One cannot advocate for Theocracy
and Democracy at the same time.
When all citizens and residents must follow
laws and precepts of one dominant religion,
regardless of individuals' beliefs or faiths,
that is not freedom; that is oppression.

Patriots uphold and defend the Constitution;
not subvert it.

Amendments Matter

Coda

Faith and Object Permanence

...for Karin

Time is both linear and cyclical; as paradoxically, change is constant. Time graduates ever forward; while ever doubling back.
"Comforting... The changing of seasons was like a patient heartbeat."

Paradox: by definition... absurd, while always true.

Uroboros

The rubble at our feet may seem to lack order.
Step back, look again.
The rocks lead to the lake.
The lake leads to the mountains.
The mountains lead to the sky and stars.
There is order and hope beyond the rubble beneath.

Look Again

Butterfly Effect- Small Causes and Large Effects

We don't live in vacuums of present.
The past is always a Cause.
The present is always future's past.
Be mindful...
Proper Thought... Proper Speech... Proper Action...

Proper Butterfly

Conversations With Karin...

To be content is to have no
need, no desire, no want.

Siddhartha said at his death,
"All component things decay.
Work hard. Seek salvation."

There are thousands of states
between Heaven and Hell.
And in each state there are
thousands more.
We can be in one or all.
Acknowledge the state.

First, acknowledge that life is
struggle and pain.
Suffering...

To be "Enlightened" is to
overcome these things, not to
ignore or forget them.

Thank you for reading
Fear Naught
The Junk Drawer of Poetry

Look for a new title in 2020
Sincerely,

Owen Patterson